In the Forest

Learning Directional Concepts

Wes Lipschultz

Math for the REAL World™

Rosen Classroom™

New York

A forest is a place with many trees and plants.

There are also many animals in the forest.

Let's look around!

Eagles live in the forest. We see an eagle above the trees.

Snakes live in the forest. We see a snake under a rock.

Squirrels live in the forest. We see a squirrel in a tree.

Owls live in the forest. We see an owl on a branch.

Deer live in the forest. We see a deer behind a tree.

Foxes live in the forest. We see a fox in front of a bush.

Rabbits live in the forest. We see a rabbit next to some flowers.

Have you ever been in a forest? What did you see?

Words to Know

branch

eagle

owl

rabbit

snake

squirrel